This Igloo book belongs to:

. . . .

. . . .

Reading Together

This story is written in a special way so that a child and an adult can 'take turns' in reading the text.

Once upon a time there were two children called Hansel and Gretel. Hansel and Gretel lived with their father and stepmother. Their father was a woodcutter. He was kind. Their stepmother was not kind at all.

Hansel and Gretel lived with their father and stepmother.

The left hand side is for the adult to read.

The right hand side has a simple sentence (taken from the story) which the child reads.

Firstly, it is always helpful to read the whole book to your child, stopping to talk about the pictures. Explain that you are going to read it again but this time the child can join in.

Read the left hand page and when you come to the sentence which is repeated on the other page run your finger under this. Your child then tries to read the same sentence opposite.

Searching for the child's sentence in the adult version is a useful activity. Your child will have a real sense of achievement when all the sentences on the right hand page can be read. Giving lots of praise is very important.

Enjoy the story together.

I Can Read...

Hansel and Gretel

Once upon a time there were two
children called Hansel and Gretel.
Hansel and Gretel lived with their
father and stepmother.
Their father was a woodcutter.
He was kind.
Their stepmother was not kind at all.

Hansel and Gretel lived with their
father and stepmother.

They were very poor.
There was no food to eat.
Hansel heard his stepmother talking
to his father.
"The children eat too much," said the
stepmother. "Take them into the woods
and leave them there. Then I can have
all the food."
Hansel thought of a plan. Hansel filled
his pockets with white stones.

Hansel filled his pockets with white stones.

The next day all the family went into the woods. As they walked, Hansel secretly dropped the white stones one at a time.

The father made a fire to keep them warm. Hansel and Gretel fell asleep by the fire.

When they woke up it was dark. They were all alone.

Hansel and Gretel fell asleep by the fire.

Hansel and Gretel followed the stones
back to their house.
Their stepmother was angry.
She took them back into the woods.
Hansel had no more stones so he
dropped breadcrumbs instead.
Hansel and Gretel fell asleep again.

Hansel and Gretel followed the stones back to their house.

When they woke up they were all alone.
The birds had eaten all the breadcrumbs.
They could not find the way home.
Hansel and Gretel found a house made
out of gingerbread and sweets.

Hansel and Gretel found a house
made out of gingerbread and sweets.

The house belonged to a wicked witch.
She pretended to be kind at first.
She gave Hansel and Gretel lovely food
to eat. But then she locked Hansel
in a cage.
The witch made Gretel do all the work.

The house belonged to
a wicked witch.

The witch gave Hansel lots of food.
"I will eat you when you are nice and
fat," she said.
Every day the witch felt Hansel's finger.
But she could not see very well.
Hansel put a twig in her hand instead
of his finger.
The witch thought Hansel was skinny.

Hansel and Gretel ran back
to their house.

Key Words

Can you read these words and find them in the book?

father

Hansel and Gretel

gingerbread house

witch

Questions and Answers

Now that you've read the story can you answer these questions?

a. Who did Hansel and Gretel live with?

b. Who did the gingerbread house belong to?

c. What did the witch lock Hansel in?

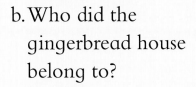

a. Father and stepmother   b. The witch   c. A cage

Tell your own Story

Can you make up a different story
with the pictures and words below?

stepmother

father

Hansel and Gretel

birds

witch

asleep

food

cage

gingerbread
house

Mix and Match

Draw a line from the pictures to the correct word to match them up.

birds

food

witch

Hansel and Gretel

gingerbread house

father